SUPER SPORTS STAR JASON KIDD

Stew Thornley

Enslow Publishers, Inc.

40 Industrial Road   PO Box 38
Box 398   Aldershot
Berkeley Heights, NJ 07922   Hants GU12 6BP
USA   UK

http://www.enslow.com

Library of Congress Cataloging-in-Publication Data

Thornley, Stew.
   Super sports star Jason Kidd / Stew Thornley.
     cm. – (Super sports star)
   Includes bibliographical references (p.) and index.
   ISBN-10: 0-7660-1806-7
   1. Kidd, Jason—Juvenile literature. 2. Basketball players—United States—
Biography—Juvenile literature. [1. Kidd, Jason. 2. Basketball players. 3. Racially
mixed people—Biography.] I. Title. II. Series.
   GV884.K53 T56   2002
   796.323'092—dc21   2001000814

ISBN-13: 978-0-7660-1806-8

Printed in the United States of America

10 9 8 7 6 5 4 3

To Our Readers: We have done our best to make sure all Internet addresses in this book were active and appropriate when we went to press. However, the author and the publisher have no control over and assume no liability for the material available on those Internet sites or on other Web sites they may link to. Any comments or suggestions can be sent by e-mail to comments@enslow.com or to the address on the back cover.

Photo Credits: Nathaniel Butler/NBAE/Getty Images, pp. 4, 41; NBA Entertainment. Photo by Sam Forencich, pp. 9, 13, 19; NBA Entertainment. Photo by Barry Gossage, pp. 17, 32, 34, 39, 45; NBA Entertainment. Photo by Andy Hayt, pp. 6, 22, 24; NBA Entertainment. Photo by Glenn James, p. 28; NBA Entertainment. Photo by Layne Murdoch, p. 26; NBA Entertainment. Photo by Sandy Tenuto, p. 11; NBA Entertainment. Photo by Noren Trotman, pp. 1, 30, 43, 46; NBA Entertainment. Photo by Rocky Widner, p. 36.

Cover Photo: Noren Trotman/NBAE/Getty Images.

CONTENTS

Introduction

Jason Kidd is a point guard for the New Jersey Nets of the National Basketball Association (NBA). A point guard's job is not just to score points. He also passes the ball to other players so they can score.

Kidd makes dazzling no-look passes just like Magic Johnson once did. But Kidd can do more. He also rebounds well for a guard. He always seems to be in the right place to grab the ball after missed shots. He does not have a great jump shot, but he still gets points. "He's a better scorer than shooter," said his first coach in college.

Some players make dunk shots the most important part of their game. But they would not be able to do it without players like Jason Kidd. The most important part of Kidd's game is his passing. He gets the ball to other players so that they can score.

Jason Kidd is a quiet person. He does not talk trash or get in anyone's face on the court. "I guess when people talk about me," he says, "they have to talk about my game."

Doing It All

Jason Kidd had five triple-doubles during the 1999–2000 season. That meant he reached double figures (10 or more) in three categories, such as points, rebounds, and assists. By the end of the year, Kidd had more triple-doubles in his career than Michael Jordan ever had.

But Kidd never had a triple-double in a playoff game. In May 2000, Kidd played for the Phoenix Suns. The Suns knew they would need a big game from Kidd. They trailed the Los Angeles Lakers, 3 games to none, in the playoffs. They had to win to keep playing.

The Suns scored 38 points in the first quarter to open up a big lead. By the end of the third quarter, Kidd had 22 points and 15 assists in the game. The Suns had such a big lead that they did not have to work quite so hard in the final quarter. Kidd did not score any more points, and he got only one more assist. But he was able to come up with a few more rebounds. With 22 points, 16 assists, and 10 rebounds,

Jason Kidd had achieved a triple-double. It was his first-ever in a playoff game.

The Suns won the game, 117–98, and were able to keep playing in the series. It was a team effort, but no member of the Suns was bigger that day than Jason Kidd.

★ UP CLOSE

Jason Kidd married Joumana Samaha in February 1997. Their son, T. J., was born in 1998. Kidd also has an older son, Jason, Jr. "They've helped me put things in perspective," Kidd said of his family. "Basketball was always the number-one thing in my life. But you realize that it's just part of your life. Joumana has really helped me understand what it takes to be a husband and a dad."

Learning His Craft

CHAPTER 2

Jason Kidd learned the value of passing the ball when he was young. He often played basketball on teams with older players. "I was always one of the youngest ones," he said. "For a long time I would be one of the last ones chosen. So I learned how to pass." Everyone wants to score, Kidd learned quickly. "I would get picked for teams a lot because they knew I wouldn't shoot." Kidd let the other players score by passing the ball to them often.

Jason Kidd was born on March 23, 1973, in San Francisco, California. He started playing basketball with older kids when he was in third grade. He played on a fourth-grade basketball team because not enough fourth-grade players had signed up.

One of the older players he played against was Gary Payton. Payton went on to become a great point guard in the NBA. Payton said he helped to toughen up Kidd. Payton and Kidd often played one-on-one against each other. Payton usually won, but it was good for Kidd.

Basketball was always Jason Kidd's best sport, even as a young boy.

"It helped me understand that if I wanted to get where Gary was, I had to work a lot harder."

Kidd grew up in Oakland, California, with his family. "Dad is black and Mom is white," he explains. "I had two different cultures and two different backgrounds to learn from. I think that helped me to be special." Kidd also has two younger sisters, Denise and Kim.

Basketball was always Kidd's best sport. By eighth grade, he was a great star. He had to hang around after games and sign autographs for the fans.

In ninth grade, he attended St. Joseph's of Notre Dame High School. The school is in Alameda, California, a city next to Oakland. Another star player on the team was Calvin Byrd. Byrd was a senior, in his last year of school, when Kidd was a freshman, in his first year. Kidd and Byrd were a great pair. Kidd passed the ball to Byrd who scored points. The fans loved it.

With Kidd and Byrd, the St. Joseph Pilots

Jason Kidd was named the best high school basketball player in the country during his senior year.

won the East Shore Athletic League title. They made it to the second round of the Northern California playoffs. They eventually lost, but it was a great season. Calvin Byrd was named to the high school All-America team. Jason Kidd was named California Freshman of the Year.

Byrd graduated, but the Pilots kept winning, thanks to Kidd. Kidd also helped the team and the school in other ways. St. Joseph sold Jason Kidd T-shirts to raise money for its athletic programs. Kidd also helped to attract sellout crowds to the St. Joseph gym for every game. In fact, St. Joseph even moved some of its games to the Oakland Coliseum. The Coliseum is where the NBA Golden State Warriors play. It can hold many more fans than a high school gym.

Kidd often passed the ball, but sometimes he kept it and scored himself. He could jump and get rebounds, but he could also jump high enough to dunk the ball himself.

St. Joseph won the California Division I

state title in 1991 and 1992. Kidd was named California Player of the Year after each of those seasons. In 1992, his senior year, Kidd won the Naismith Award as the best high school player in the country.

In April 1992, Kidd played in the McDonald's All-America Game in Atlanta, Georgia. He played with some of the best players in the country. Having great players to pass to helped him earn even more assists. One of the players on Kidd's team was Othella Harrington. The game was a great experience for Kidd. "It was a thrill to play with someone like Othella, who could dominate the game every minute he was in," said Kidd. Part of the reason Harrington did so well was because of the passes he got from Kidd.

★★★ UP CLOSE

Jason Kidd's hobbies include listening to music. He likes rhythm and blues. His favorite performers are the Isley Brothers and Chante Moore.

Kidd also played with other good players who could turn his passes into points. They were college players. When he was in high school, Kidd went to the University of California's gym. He practiced and played pickup games with the California players.

A lot of colleges were trying to get Kidd to play basketball for their team. But Kidd liked what he saw at California. He liked the players he practiced with there and decided he would like to have them as teammates. Jason Kidd was going to stay close to home. He was going to be a member of the California Golden Bears.

College
Days

The California Golden Bears were not a very good team in 1991–92. They won only 10 games and lost 18, but that was before Jason Kidd joined the team. California coach Lou Campanelli knew the Bears could be better. He also knew that the fans would enjoy watching Kidd. "He does things on the fast break that will bring you right out of your seat."

California knew its arena was not big enough to hold all the fans that would come to see Kidd. They moved some of the games to the larger Oakland Coliseum. It was the same thing that Kidd's high school had done. Once again, many people came to see Kidd play.

The Golden Bears improved in 1992–93. The team made it to the NCAA Tournament, which is the most important national college competition. California's first opponent in the tournament was Louisiana State. The game was a close one. It was tied with only seconds remaining. Kidd had the ball and he drove into the lane. Geert Hammink, a seven-foot player,

While in college, Jason Kidd perfected many of the skills he uses today in the NBA.

stood in his way. Kidd twisted and tossed up a shot with his right hand. It went in with one second left, and California won the game.

Next came Duke, the defending national champion. No one gave the Golden Bears much of a chance to beat Duke. But California got off to a great start. Kidd fired an alley-oop pass to Lamond Murray. Murray grabbed the ball and dunked it for a 2–0 lead. Then Kidd stole the ball and got it to K. J. Roberts. Roberts dunked the ball.

The Golden Bears led by 18 points in the second half. But Duke came back. With a little over two minutes to play, Duke was ahead by a point. Kidd drove along the baseline. He tried to pass to Murray, but the pass was blocked. It rolled into a group of players, and everyone scrambled for the loose ball. It squirted out and Kidd picked it up. He put up a shot that went in. California took the lead again, and this time they held on to it. The Golden Bears had upset Duke.

California lost its next game. But it had been a great season for the team and for Jason Kidd. He set a freshman record for most steals in a season. Kidd was voted Freshman of the Year in the Pacific 10 Conference.

As a sophomore, in his second year, he led the nation in assists. He was also named to the All-America team. The Golden Bears did well again. However, they were knocked out of the NCAA Tournament in the first round.

A New Challenge

Jason Kidd was improving each year. After two years in college, he felt he was ready for the NBA.

The Dallas Mavericks had the second pick in the 1994 NBA draft. The draft is the way that NBA teams pick new players each year. The Mavericks thought their best choices would be Jason Kidd or Grant Hill of Duke. One of the Mavericks players, Jamal Mashburn, hoped it would be Kidd. Mashburn knew he would be able to score more points with a player like Kidd passing him the ball. Mashburn got his wish when the Mavericks picked Jason Kidd.

Dallas had not played well the year before. But the Mavericks improved a great deal when Kidd joined them. In addition to Jason Kidd and Jamal Mashburn, the Mavericks had another fine player in Jimmy Jackson. The trio became know as the 3 Js—Jason, Jamal, and Jimmy.

It was Jason Kidd's job to get the ball to Mashburn and Jackson. If he could score points himself that would be great. But Dallas was more interested in his passing skills.

Kidd showed all his skills in his first game—he almost had a triple-double. Kidd finished with 10 points, 11 assists, and 9 rebounds. He was on target with his passes. Helped by Kidd, Jackson scored 37 points, and Mashburn had 30. The Mavericks beat the New Jersey Nets.

"He's the reason they won," the Nets' Armon Gilliam said about Kidd. "He makes it so easy to score by giving them passes so close to the basket. He's a special player, I can see it right now."

The Dallas Mavericks picked Jason Kidd in 1994.

Kidd really heated up during the final two months of the season. He was named the NBA Rookie of the Month in March. In early April, he had his first triple-double in the NBA. The Mavericks beat the Lakers, 130–111. Kidd had 19 points, 12 assists, and 10 rebounds. In the Mavericks' next game, Kidd had another triple-double.

A few games later, he was really great. Dallas beat Houston in double overtime. Overtime is time added to the end of a game if there is a tie score. Double overtime means two extra periods are needed to decide the winner of the game. Kidd connected for 8 three-point baskets. Three of them came in the final minute of the first overtime period. The Rockets had built an 11-point lead in overtime.

But Kidd's great shooting kept the Mavericks in the game. His three-point basket with 2.5 seconds left tied the game and forced a second overtime period. Dallas went on to win, 156–147.

Jason Kidd takes winning very seriously.

Kidd had 38 points in the game. He also had 11 rebounds, 10 assists, and 8 steals. With just two more steals, Kidd would have had a quadruple-double. A quadruple-double happens when a player has double figures (10 or more) in any four categories. That's one of the rarest feats in basketball.

Dallas did not make the playoffs. But with Jason Kidd's help, the Mavericks won 23 more games than they had in 1993–94.

In a year in which there were many great first-year players, Jason Kidd stood out. He and Grant Hill of the Detroit Pistons tied in the voting for the NBA Rookie of the Year. It was a great start for Jason Kidd, but it was only the beginning.

Getting Past the Rough Spots

Before the start of the 1995–96 season, Jason Kidd had worked hard to improve his outside shooting—shots taken far away from the basket. "I also want to stress I've worked hard to improve my passing, my defense, and my play in all other areas. When Coach [Dick] Motta wants me to score, I want the ball. But when other people are scoring, I will get them the ball," he said.

Dallas won its first four games of the season. But then the Mavericks struggled for much of the year. Jamal Mashburn hurt his knee early in the season and missed the rest of the year. Jimmy Jackson was coming back from a serious ankle injury that still slowed him down.

Kidd continued to have outstanding performances. In a game against Phoenix on January 12, Kidd had 33 points, 16 assists, and 12 rebounds. He grabbed a rebound and put up an off-balance shot in the final seconds. The shot went in, sending the game into overtime. It was Kidd's second triple-double of the year. The next night, he had his third triple-double of the year.

Near the end of the month, Kidd had a huge game. He had 21 points, 15 assists, and 16 rebounds against the Los Angeles Clippers. He was named NBA Player of the Week for the week of January 29 to February 4. A few days after that, Kidd set a Dallas record with 25 assists in a game against Utah.

Jason Kidd had many great games with the Dallas Mavericks before being traded to the Phoenix Suns.

He was voted by the fans to start for the Western Conference in the All-Star Game. Kidd finished the season with 16.6 points per game and 9.7 assists per game. His assist total was second best in the NBA.

Despite the great year by Kidd, Dallas missed the playoffs for the sixth straight year.

Less than two months into the 1996–97 season, the Mavericks traded Jason Kidd to the Phoenix Suns. The Suns needed help. The team had started the season with thirteen straight losses.

Having Kidd on their team made them better. The Suns even made the playoffs. Kidd played in 33 games for Phoenix during the regular season. The Suns won 24 of those games.

Kidd averaged 9 assists per game. That was the fourth-best total in the NBA. He did even better in the playoffs. The Suns lost in the first round of the playoffs, but Kidd had helped to get them there.

Jason Kidd helped get the Phoenix Suns to the playoffs in the 1996–97 and 1997–98 seasons.

Jason Kidd shined again in 1997–98. By midseason, the Suns had one of the best records in the NBA. Seven Phoenix players were averaging more than 10 points per game. That shows how often Kidd was getting the ball to them.

Kidd played in the All-Star Game again. He played less than half the game and still had 9 assists.

Kidd was second best in the NBA in assists per game. He had more than 700 assists and 500 rebounds. Only two other players had ever done that more than once. Those players were two of the greatest guards ever, Magic Johnson and Oscar Robertson.

The Suns made the playoffs. But, for the second year in a row, they were defeated in the first round. Jason Kidd had helped the Suns improve. Now he wanted to help them get further in the playoffs.

Pouring It On

Kidd had to wait for the 1998–99 season to start, and it was a long wait. There was a dispute between the players and the team owners, and the first part of the season was cancelled.

When the season finally started in February, Kidd was ready. On February 15, he had a triple-double in a win over Denver. He had another triple-double two nights later. The following week, Kidd was sick. He had the flu and he felt dizzy. He left the game in the first quarter, but he came back and got another triple-double. Three nights later, he was still sick but he got a triple-double anyway.

Kidd finished the season with 7 triple-doubles, the most in the NBA. Kidd was named the NBA Player of the Month in April. He ended up leading the league in assists per game. He increased his scoring average to 16.9 points and averaged nearly 7 rebounds per game. He was fourth in the NBA in steals.

Kidd was clearly one of the best all-around

Jason Kidd was a member of the gold-medal winning Olympic team in the 2000 Olympics.

players in the league. He was named to the All-NBA team.

It was a great year for Jason Kidd, but it ended again in disappointment. The Suns were knocked out of the playoffs in the first round.

Kidd received a big honor during the off-season. He was named to the United States Olympic team. The team played in a tournament in the summer of 1999. The Olympics held in Australia in 2000, brought Jason Kidd and the rest of the American team a gold medal.

In the meantime, Kidd played in the 2000 All-Star Game. This time it was a special treat. The game was played in Oakland, Kidd's hometown. He led all players with 14 assists. One was a spectacular alley-oop pass late in the game. Kidd tossed an underhanded pass high in the air. Kobe Bryant leaped high, caught it, and slammed it through the basket. Earlier, Kidd had tried another alley-oop pass. This one bounced off the backboard and through the basket. Kidd was trying to pass, not score on the play. He was as surprised as anyone when the ball went in.

Kidd was having another great year, and so were the Suns. But trouble struck in March. Kidd took an inbounds pass and drove down the right sideline. Jason Williams of Sacramento stood in his way. Kidd stopped, lost the ball, and turned to reach for it. He fell to the ground, holding his leg. He had broken his ankle. He would not be able to play for at least the rest of the regular season.

Even though he missed the final month, Kidd still had five triple-doubles for the season. That tied him for the most in the NBA with Sacramento's Chris Webber. Kidd also led the NBA in assists per game for the second year in a row.

Phoenix made the playoffs, but Kidd missed the first few games. Phoenix led San Antonio, two games to one, but needed three wins to move on. Kidd was back for the fourth game.

He had 9 points and 10 assists, as the Suns won the game.

The Suns moved on to the next round where they were beaten by the Los Angeles Lakers. Their season was over, but they had finally made it past the first round of the playoffs.

In 2000–01, Kidd played more great basketball. He led the league in assists for the third year in a row. He scored a lot of points, too. In one game, late in the season, Kidd scored 43 points against the Houston Rockets.

Kidd looked forward to another good year in 2001–02. But, he would be

Jason Kidd goes up for a shot over the outstretched arms of his defender.

doing it with a new team. In July 2001, Phoenix traded Kidd to the New Jersey Nets.

Kidd enjoys other sports, including golf. He is also active in his community. He is on the board of directors for the Boys and Girls Clubs in Phoenix. He also contributes to his hometown. Every Thanksgiving, he and other NBA players from the Oakland area provide meals for homeless people.

Kidd has formed the Jason Kidd Foundation. It provides money for children's medical research. He has a fan club, called "Kidd's Klub." All the money raised by the fan club goes to the Jason Kidd Foundation.

Jason Kidd appears to fly through the air as he goes up for a shot.

CAREER STATISTICS

Team	Year	GP	FG%	FT%	Reb.	Ast.	Stl.	Blk.	Pts.	PPG
NBA										
Dallas	1994–1995	79	.385	.698	430	607	151	24	922	11.7
Dallas	1995–1996	81	.381	.692	553	783	175	26	1,348	16.6
Dallas	1996–1997	22	.369	.667	90	200	45	8	217	9.9
Phoenix	1996–1997	33	.423	.688	159	296	79	12	382	11.6
Phoenix	1997–1998	82	.416	.799	510	745	162	26	954	11.6
Phoenix	1998–1999	50	.444	.757	339	539	114	19	846	16.9
Phoenix	1999–2000	67	.409	.829	483	678	134	28	959	14.3
Phoenix	2000–2001	77	.411	.814	494	753	166	23	1,299	16.9
New Jersey	2001–2002	82	.391	.814	595	808	175	20	1,208	14.7
New Jersey	2002–2003	80	.414	.841	504	711	179	25	1,495	18.7
New Jersey	2003–2004	67	.384	.827	428	618	122	14	1,036	15.5
New Jersey	2004–2005	66	.398	.740	488	545	123	9	951	14.4
New Jersey	2005–2006	80	.404	.795	580	672	150	29	1,065	13.3
Totals		**866**	**.402**	**.780**	**5,653**	**7,955**	**1,775**	**263**	**12,682**	**14.6**

GP—Games Played
FG%—Field Goal Percentage
FT%—Free Throw Percentage

Reb.—Rebounds
Ast.—Assists
Stl.—Steals

Blk.—Blocked Shots
Pts.—Points Scored
PPG—Points per Game

Where to Write to Jason Kidd

Mr. Jason Kidd
New Jersey Nets
390 Murray Hill Parkway
East Rutherford, NJ
07073

Jason Kidd has many talents on the basketball court.

WORDS TO KNOW

alley-oop—A pass thrown toward the basket. It is intended for a teammate to take the pass in the air and dunk the ball.

assist—A pass to a teammate who scores.

double-teaming—Putting two defenders on one player.

draft—The way that NBA teams choose new players each year.

dunk—A shot that is slammed through the basket from directly above the basket. Also known as a slam or slam dunk.

freshman—A first-year student in high school or college.

jump shot—A shot taken while jumping.

NCAA Tournament—The national college tournament. NCAA stands for National Collegiate Athletic Association.

no-look pass—A pass made in one direction while looking in another direction.

outside shot—A shot taken far away from the basket.

playmaker—The player who directs the team's offense.

quadruple-double—Getting double figures (10 or more) in four categories.

rebound—Getting the ball after a missed shot.

senior—A student in the last year of high school or college.

sophomore—A student in the second year of high school or college.

triple-double—Getting double figures (10 or more) in three categories.

triple-teaming—Putting three defenders on a player.

Jason Kidd drives to the basket past his defender.

Jason Kidd hosts basketball camps for kids every summer.

READING ABOUT

Books

Brant, James. *Jason Kidd*. Broomall, Pa.: Chelsea House Publishers, 1997.

Brown, Jerry and Mike Tulmello. *Jason Kidd: Rising Sun*. Champaign, Il.: Sports Publishing, Inc., 1999.

Roessing, Walter. "Meet Mr. Nice Guy," *Boys' Life*, January 1996, p. 20.

Whittaker, Andrea N. "Get the Point!" *Sports Illustrated for Kids*, June 1, 1999, p. 64.

Internet Addresses

The Official Web Site of the NBA
    <http://nba.com/playerfile/jason_kidd.html>

The Official Web Site of the New Jersey Nets
    <http://nba.com/nets/>

INDEX